The Adventures of Snowwoman

based on a story by
V. Suteev

The Adventures of Snowwoman

retold and illustrated by

Katya Arnold

Holiday House · New York

It was the day before Christmas. All the neighborhood children had worked hard putting up the decorations. But they had no tree! So they wrote Santa a letter.

Now they needed someone to take the letter to Santa. And they knew just who to ask.

They ran outside, bringing seven shiny apples, a carrot, and a stewpot. Then all the children got busy. Their dog, Buddy, helped. When they finished, they stepped back to admire their work.

There stood a big, beautiful Snowwoman.

"Snowwoman! Snowwoman! Take our letter to Santa and bring us back a tree! Hurry! Hurry!"

"But a storm is coming! And Santa lives beyond the scary woods!" cried Snowwoman. "I'll get lost!"

"Don't worry," said Buddy. "I'll protect you!"
"Thank you," said Snowwoman. So off they went.

They walked and walked through the forest. It was snowing, the wind was blowing, and Buddy and Snowwoman were as lost as lost could be.

Suddenly Rabbit jumped out of the bushes. "Help," cried Rabbit, "Fox is after me!"

Buddy barked at the poor rabbit and chased it into the woods. Then Fox ran by, saying, "Where's my rabbit?"

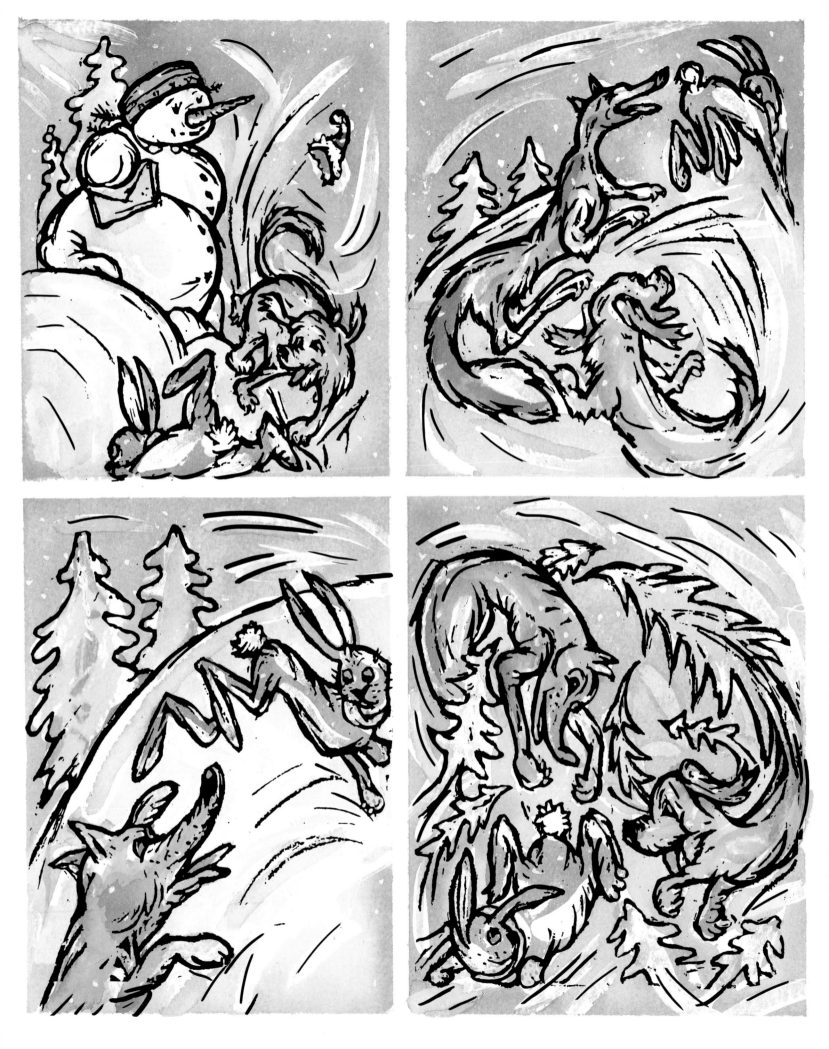

Snowwoman was all alone. She held the letter tight, struggling against the howling wind and swirling snow. The storm got worse, and before long poor Snowwoman collapsed. There was nothing left of her but seven shiny apples, one carrot, and a stewpot.

Fox crept back and said, "Where is that dog who scared off my rabbit?" When Fox looked around, she saw the letter on the ground. She grabbed it and ran away.

Buddy came back. When he saw what had happened to Snowwoman, he sat down and cried and cried.

Rabbit and his friends teased him. "Cry, puppy, cry! You deserve it for chasing Rabbit!"

"I'm sorry!" said Buddy. "I promise I'll never scare Rabbit again!"

"Well, in that case, stop crying," said Rabbit. "We'll help you get your friend back."

The squirrels helped, too.

They all got to work, tails wagging and paws flying.
Soon Snowwoman was as good as new, with most of her
shiny apples, much of her carrot, and all of her stewpot.

"Thank you, thank you, thank you," said Snowwoman.
"But where is the letter?"

The letter was nowhere to be found. Snowwoman said,
"But without a letter, Santa won't give me the tree!
What will I do?"

Then Magpie appeared and stuttered, "Here is the
lle-ttt-ter, here is the lle-ttt-ter!"

"Where did you find it?" asked Buddy.

"Oh, my!" said Magpie. "That's a story!" And they
listened as she told them all about it.

"Now we have the letter," said Snowwoman. "But I still don't know how to find Santa!"

Rabbit said, "Uh-oh. Only Bear knows that."

So off they went to ask Bear for help.

Bear was sound asleep so they had to shout to wake him.
"Get up, Bear! Rise and shine, Bear! We need to find Santa.
Christmas is almost here!"

Bear said, "In that case, I better help you!"
"Hurry," said Snowwoman. "There's no time to lose."
And they rushed off, looking for Santa.
Snowwoman was trying so hard that she…

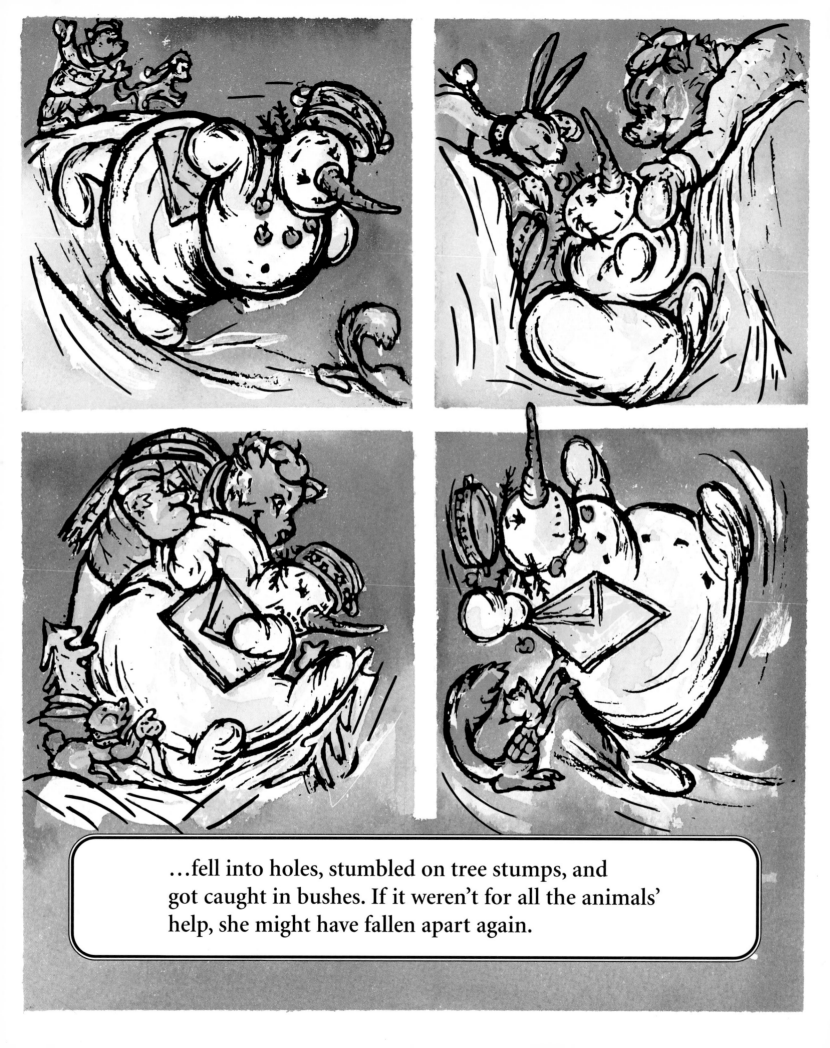

…fell into holes, stumbled on tree stumps, and got caught in bushes. If it weren't for all the animals' help, she might have fallen apart again.

Finally they reached Santa. But after Santa read the
letter he said, "You're too late! I'm all ready to go."

The animals pleaded with him. When they told
Santa about Snowwoman's adventures, and how she
had fallen apart in the storm, he said, "What a
brave Snowwoman you are! And what good friends
you have. I'll help you."

So Santa tied his most beautiful tree to the sleigh. Snowwoman and Buddy climbed on, too, shouting, "Thank you, Bear! Thank you, rabbits! Thank you, squirrels! Have a very Merry Christmas!"

Then Santa took Snowwoman and Buddy right to the children's home, his first stop of the night.

And Bear went back to sleep.